SACKED BY THE QUARTERBACK

AN ENEMIES TO LOVERS MM SPORTS ROMANCE

THE LOCKER ROOM PLAYBOOKS
BOOK 1

RYLEY BANKS

Published by Three Lemon Press, LLC

ISBN: 978-1-962835-07-7 (ebook) 978-1-962835-08-4 (paperback)

Editing by Amy Briggs with Briggs Consulting LLC

Cover Design by Rachel Christley of The Author Buddy

For everyone who's always wondered if football players check out their teammates in those pants...

CONTENT ADVISORY

Content advisories for all of Ryley's books are available here: https://ryleybanks.com/books/contentwarn ings/

There are two ways you can use this section:
1)   As a list of things to avoid;
OR
2)   As a menu of things to look forward to.

I trust you to know yourself. Happy reading either way.

xoxo Ryley

CHAPTER
ONE
PAUL

I SHOVED myself into the huddle with the rest of the offense, breath steaming from under our face masks in the cold October air. My lungs burned as I sucked in oxygen, but my cheeks flamed in disgrace.

"Clock's running out and we're only down by seven points, so we've gotta make a move." Quarterback Will MacLeod jabbed a gloved finger at the other wide receiver then turned to me. "Martell, the ball's coming to you *if* you can get out in front of your defender. They won't expect it after you couldn't get your hands on the last one. Think you can take what I give you? 'Cause it's coming hard." He gave me a cocked-eyebrow grin with that fucking awful double-entendre challenge.

I ground my teeth so violently they creaked as the rest of the offense in the huddle whooped over the screaming crowd, fake-scandalized. But the desperation that had haunted the offensive line since late in the third quarter finally broke.

Not that I'd tell him, but MacLeod's plan was a good move, especially for a second string QB and a walk-on. And it'd give me a chance to redeem myself after I'd fucked up, starting too late down the field and barely touching the ball as I failed to catch his pass.

That asshole was on his knees in front of us—how many times had I pictured him in this exact position? So I crowded over him until he looked up. My blood thundered with testosterone as we stared at each other.

"Anything you give me, I can handle," I replied. The huddle erupted with laughter again. I bared my teeth and shoved my mouth guard back in.

MacLeod's green eyes flashed. "You'd better, Martell," he said around a too-cocky grin. "Or your ass is mine."

My face burned for an entirely different reason.

The huddle broke and I lined up wide right. Everything depended on this catch—State U winning the homecoming game against our conference rivals, for one. Securing my athletic scholarship for another year. Giving my parents bragging rights at the next family get-together. And, oh yeah, whether ESPN's talking heads would later be babbling about "junior wide receiver Paul Martell's butter fingers" or "Martell's impossible game-winning catch."

Little would they know that my mistake earlier had less to do with my skills and more to do with the epic distraction that was Will *motherfucking* MacLeod.

My world narrowed to the game. The ball snapped. I sprinted toward the endzone. Eight yards down, I angled across the field, losing the defender chasing me entirely. I whipped my head to MacLeod.

Damn. He'd done it. The pass was fucking perfect. Released just as he got pummeled into the turf.

I leaped, vaulting over an opposing player who dropped low to take out my knees.

My hands locked around the football, and I cradled it into my body. Secure. It *had* to be.

I slammed into the ground, breath punched out of me—

Clouds hung in the blue sky between the gaps in my helmet's face mask, the roar of the crowd the only thing louder than my ragged breaths. In the middle of an out-of-body experience, I sat up, and my arms unlocked around the ball still clenched in my grip.

Touchdown.

One of our guys yanked me to my feet and pulled me into a sweaty hug, yelling and smashing our helmets together. When I pulled away, my eyes—goddamn traitors—searched out Will.

Had he been watching me?

I was being ridiculous—he threw a pass to a precise location dictated by the play, trusting I'd do my job and be exactly where I needed to be. Then he got creamed into nothing by a linebacker. Of course he wasn't watching. But my stomach knotted in hope like a teenage girl obsessing over her crush noticing her walking down a flight of stairs or some shit.

The touchdown I'd caught had run out the clock, leaving us down by one point, and Will was already regrouping at the three-yard line for the go-ahead for the two-point conversion. My chest tightened, and I clenched my jaw. What the fuck did it matter what he thought? *Get it together, Martell. Game's not over.*

I assembled with the rest of the offense, still reluctantly impressed with the play Will executed. As good, if not better, than our starting quarterback would've if it weren't for a potentially season-ending knee injury.

My body moved on autopilot when the ball left our center's hands to fly to Will. But I'd just made a major play, and their defense was on me like flies on shit. Time slowed as Will assessed the receivers, and then...

That crazy motherfucker ran the ball *himself*.

The score was barely final when the screaming home team fans rushed the field in a raging river of blue and white. For a moment, I was able to savor our victory, forgetting about my missed catch and that I'd almost cost us the win, and instead focus on the game-winning touchdown I'd pulled in.

Cooldown and media interviews passed in a blur. It seemed like everyone wanted a piece of me and Will. Thankfully, we were interviewed together only once. I managed to answer questions without tripping over my own tongue, and solidly kept my temper in check when asked by one guy about my missed incomplete pass.

But God, the way Will handled himself—his easy-going California cool-guy charm had them eating up every sound bite, especially when he told the media he was hoping his mom was watching. I left for the locker room as soon as I could.

The media finally gone, we all cut loose. Whooping and yelling, banging on the lockers and benches, my teammates chest bumping each other and smashing helmets. Sports drink bottles flew through the musky, humid air, the energy practically vibrating off the walls.

I forced more enthusiasm than I felt. We'd fought hard for the win and deserved every bit of praise. At least everyone else did. My mistake had almost cost us the game, and I'd certainly hear about it from Coach. But I already knew an error like that couldn't happen again.

Shouldn't have happened in the first place.

I grinned and congratulated my teammates, glancing around for Will. But he and his surfer boy good looks were nowhere to be found.

"Martell, you heading out with us?" one of the linebackers asked. I laughed and shook my head, appreciating the invitation.

"Got a big project due Monday," I lied smoothly while I took off my sweaty padding. I was doing fine in my classes, which made me a genius in the eyes of some of the guys on the team. As I suspected, nobody questioned my excuse. I held out my fist to him, and he bumped it. "Get some for me, yeah?"

"You know it, man."

Because of the press interviews, I hadn't had a chance to come down from the energy from the game, and I needed a distraction. The university had invested millions in the state-of-the-art training facility, so I headed through the well-lit maze of blue, white, and shiny, chrome detailing to the well-stocked refueling station. I killed a bottle of Gatorade and a couple of the peanut butter protein bars that tasted like actual food.

Temporarily sated, I shucked the rest of my uniform. I grabbed my shower stuff, wrapped a towel tightly around my waist, and headed to clean up.

Most of the guys had showered and were already changing to go out to dinner, then on to the afterparty—the *real* celebration. Sweaty bodies, muscles flexing, backs arching, then satisfied for the rest of the night.

My teammates would be hooking up with their preferred version of Tits McGee, but my chosen partner would be more...Dick McDude. I never made it a secret that I was gay, and most of the team didn't give a shit. More than a few friends had tried to hook me up over the past few years—not *un*appreciated. But I hated how gossip ran through teams faster than wildfire, so I kept any dating life—or lack thereof—private. Back in high school, some asshole outed my crush on another student during practice. That was more than enough to teach me to play my cards close to my chest from then on.

And if the current fantasy guy in my spank bank happened to look a little too much like Will MacLeod, well... The team didn't need more drama, so I'd be keeping *that* to myself too.

Just as I entered the showers, Will materialized out of the steam like some god, heading directly toward me.

I did *not* allow myself to look down at where his white towel hit his waist, so I focused on his upper half, which was arguably more distracting. His shaggy blond hair, still wet from his shower, had darkened, the water dripping from the waves onto his shoulders. A droplet slid over his collarbone and down his pecs. I caught myself staring a moment too late, and his green eyes met mine.

He was tailormade to torture me. I crushed my eyelids shut.

"MacLeod," I called as he passed by. Jesus Christ. What was I even doing? I had no plan. But my mouth didn't seem to know that.

"Hey, bro," he said. "Awesome catch today. Totally came in clutch." The bright, open friendliness on his face took me off guard. His teeth flashed in a grin, white and straight, as his lips tilted up—were they as soft as they looked? Fuck.

Other than in practice, we'd barely said two words to each other since Will had walked onto the team this season. Not that he hadn't tried. But avoiding a blond, green-eyed teammate who'd crawled straight out of my wet dreams seemed to be in my best interest at the time.

"You got a minute? After I shower?" I asked. Shit, that wasn't supposed to come out.

"Sure thing. Be a few anyway—gotta get changed."

Before he could say anything else, I stomped off, took the first available shower stall, and cranked the water as hot as it would go, losing myself in the misty haze.

Fuck me, this was getting out of hand. Thank god I was in there behind a curtain because my dick had decided it very much wanted to be *in* hand. "Oh, no you don't," I whispered to it. I was losing my mind.

It was one thing to be attracted to Will. He was objectively hot. Miles of tanned skin, a body chiseled from the same brutal conditioning regimen the whole team went through. He and I were pretty evenly matched in height, an idea my brain liked to toy with. Would he press me into a wall, biting my neck, rutting against me until we both spilled, warm and wet, all over each other's abs? I'd already seen him kneel, but how would he look with my hand gripped in his soft-looking hair and his lips stretched wide around me...

The dude was fire.

But even worse, he was someone I could see myself dating, if we weren't teammates playing for a Division I school. Relationships could tear teams apart, screwing with dynamics, undoing seasons of trust and progression, and forcing the other players to choose sides like the kids of shitty divorced parents.

What sucked the most was how Will had tried to be friends early on, after he'd officially made the team. Talking to me, teasing...maybe even flirting? I'd brushed him off every time, but that didn't mean I didn't watch him every chance I got. I couldn't help myself. But why get close, take the risk, set myself up for distraction and heartbreak? And his sweet, earnest face when I talked to him now...

Enough.

I turned the water to cold, and my body exploded in shivers and goosebumps. Half of my shower was scrubbing off the game sweat. The other half was waiting for my dick to soften.

By the time I'd dried off and slung the towel around myself, I was mostly convinced I could manage to act like a normal human for the time it would take to get dressed and get the hell out of there. Will probably forgot I'd stupidly asked him to stay and was long gone anyway.

No such luck.

He lounged on the padded bench in front of his locker area, one ankle crossed carelessly over the other knee as he watched something on his phone. Goddammit, it's like he wanted me to look at his crotch. Tight jeans hugged thick thighs, and his upper body was covered by a black tee and a leather jacket that fit better than it had any right to. And the fact that I blushed only irritated me.

"Hey, Paul," he said. "What did you want from me?"

And wasn't that a loaded question?

"You think you're hot shit, but you've got a lot to prove," I spat out, my mouth totally running away from me. "You only played today because of Washington's injury, and that pass of yours almost cost us the game. Glad you managed to get it together or we'd be screwed."

Hurt and confusion shuttered his face. It was like every emotion from him blasted into me, magnified a hundred times, and I couldn't look at him anymore, his wounded expression.

"Fuck you. I know I'm not the starting QB." Will stood up and crossed his arms around his chest. "But I earned my spot. And the incomplete pass..." Will trailed off, shaking his head as he turned his phone screen toward me. The blood drained from my face as the video replay only confirmed what I already knew.

All my fault—I was too busy watching you move, and I started down the field a split-second too late. But, like the asshole I was, I kept my mouth shut.

Will drew in a deep breath. "I thought—I thought you and I were in synch out there today, especially for that last play. And when you asked me to wait here for you, I thought, just for a second..." His arms tightened around his chest, just slightly, the jacket pulling around his broad shoulders. "You know what? Forget it. Guess I was wrong."

"Guess so." I clamped my jaw closed, swallowing hard

against any other defense mechanisms that wanted to show up.

Will looked me straight in the face, emerald eyes hard. "I take it you're not coming out with us?"

"Nope. I don't need you."

Will clenched his hands into fists before he turned and stormed to the exit, leaving me staring after him in my damp towel. My eyes followed him until the door slammed behind him. I swiped a hand over my face, oily regret pouring through me. What the fuck had I done?

CHAPTER
TWO

WILL

THE OUTSIDE DOORS slid shut behind me as I left the stadium, locker room, and Paul Martell behind. *What is his deal? And why do I even care?*

I scoffed. Of course he didn't need me. But this was the second time he'd said that, phrased it that way. The reader in me couldn't help but remember the quote from Shakespeare's *Hamlet*: "The lady doth protest too much, methinks."

I picked up my pace, heading away from the stadium and toward the restaurant the team had chosen for the post-game celebration, trying desperately not to think about Paul standing there in a while towel, water dripping down the carved planes of his chest. Instead, my mind slid to the previous few months with the team.

———

Two months ago

Humid early August heat billowed around us, the air and the eagerness equally tangible as we cooled down and hydrated.

"...Lawrence, Zaya, Abbott..."

Come on, come on. Please let him say my name. My train of thought was running out of control, but to the casual observer, I was as cool as a cucumber. No fidgeting, no swaying, just cool indifference. My mother's much-repeated advice, the same thing she'd told me years ago when Dad died and cruel kids used that against me, reverberated in my mind as though she were right there. *Never let them know they affect you.*

"...Bolden, MacLeod..."

The tension melted from my muscles, and I didn't hear anything else until the coach put down his tablet and looked around the group of sweaty dudes. "Congratulations," he said. "You live to see another day. Let's see if you survive practicing with the team. If I didn't read your name off, you won't be playing for the Rams."

After a few weeks of strength and conditioning and tryouts, what had started as a group of probably seventy-five prospective unrecruited walk-ons for the football team had been whittled down to less than ten.

I wanted to believe I'd had a better shot than most, transferring to State U for this semester from a Division III school where I was the starting quarterback. I could do agility drills and run 40s in my sleep. And maybe I did have a better chance—but I wasn't on scholarship, and the next day I'd be suiting up with the rest of the team to prove myself all over again.

Some of the team, including starters, had even showed up to watch the tryouts. Most were guys who anyone would instantly clock as football players, but one dude could have been a Calvin Klein model, and I unfortunately hadn't even seen him with his clothes off. His dark tan skin glowed in contrast to the college-logoed light gray hoodie he wore, which was stretched to capacity around his wide shoulders. Nearly black hair swept across his forehead, almost too short to run my fingers through. And his eyes, a stunning gray, were locked on me.

I'd seen the roster online, and his eyes gave him away—Paul Martell, one of the starting wide receivers. Talented, a junior like me, and, unless I was way off in my assessment, he liked what he saw. And I didn't mean my passing skills—more like my tight end.

With a short nod, Martell got up off the bench and headed out. Didn't matter. I'd meet him soon enough.

I stripped off my sweaty pads and stretched before grabbing a Gatorade and fist-bumping the other dudes who made the cut.

"MacLeod!" Bernard, one of the offensive coaches, jogged up to me as I was unwrapping a protein bar. I swiped sweaty dark blond hair away from my forehead and squinted in the bright sun to see him better.

"Coach was watching today. Got quite an arm on you." Bernard gestured over his shoulder to the head coach before he scrolled on the tablet sandwiched in the crook of his arm. A hint of farmer tan peeked out from his shirt sleeve. "Originally from California, and transferred here from a D-III school as a junior, huh? Gave up a starting slot to shoot your shot here?"

I stood up a little taller. "Yep. I wasn't on scholarship there either and State U's closer to home now."

Bernard cocked an eyebrow, but I didn't elaborate.

"Well," he said, "Coach likes what he sees. Gave me the go-ahead to officially get you on the roster."

Holy shit. "Thanks, Bernard." My stomach did happy flips like an excited dolphin.

"We'll see how you fit when you practice with the team. Oh, and stop by ResLife, they'll get you situated. Congratulations, kid. You're officially a Ram."

*

"So, how did it go?" Even the tiny phone speaker couldn't drown out the excitement in my mom's voice. I'd texted her after I hit up ResLife to let her know I had news, and she'd called right away. Anyone else I'd let go to voicemail, but never her.

"I'm on the team, Mom. I'm hella stoked."

"Will, that's wonderful! When's your first game?"

I chuckled, enjoying her enthusiasm, and sat in the shade on a low retaining wall around some flower beds to give her my full attention. "Slow your roll, Mom.

Tomorrow I practice with the team for the first time. We'll go from there."

"Show them what you got. You always make me proud, no matter what."

A lump formed in my throat, and I pictured her drawing me into a hug, encouraging me to stoop so she could kiss my forehead. I'd outpaced my mom in both height and bulk since I was twelve, but she was always a spitfire, doing what needed to get done, especially since Dad passed a decade ago. Since then, it had been just the two of us.

"I—I even got housing. I'm moving in this afternoon." I swallowed tightly, eyes burning. "No academic scholarship, but they sent me to ResLife and they're covering my room and board in the athlete complex. It's sweet AF and right across from the shitty dorms I've been in for the summer session." I still couldn't believe it—my brain totally glitched when the housing adviser told me.

"Give me your new address when you're settled. I want to send a welcome care package."

"You got it." I adjusted the phone in my hand as I laid down on the grass. "So, now that the news is out of the way…what did you think of chapter seventeen?"

"When the duke finally hooks up with his valet? I was fanning myself so much I thought it was a hot flash."

When I was a senior in high school, I'd unwisely teased Mom about reading romance novels. I believe I used the word "trashy." Surprisingly, she wasn't angry, and insisted I read one before I judged them. I'd already come out to her a couple years before, and she'd doubled down by finding LGBTQIA+ romances to read together, chapter by chapter, a book club of two. She was right—I loved them as much as she did, reveling in happily-ever-afters with couples who looked like me.

We discussed our current read for a while longer—how the men were almost caught together on the balcony when the duke left the ball early, and how neither of us saw the duke's sister's betrayal coming. Soon, the sun had shifted enough that I checked the time. Mom must have noticed it too.

"Okay, sweetheart, I'll let you get started packing. I've got to work my side hustle and prep for an open house tomorrow." After Dad died, we were priced out of living in California and had to move. Until then, Mom only had one job—middle school math teacher. But ever since I was old enough to stay home on my own—and since my football leagues and training got more expensive—she'd gotten her real estate license to supplement.

"Sell those houses," I said. "Love you."

"Love you too."

I headed back to my old dorm, every step a little lighter. Things were looking up for Will MacLeod.

*

"Fuck!" I wheezed, desperately sucking in a breath around my spasming diaphragm. I hadn't been sacked like that in a practice in…never. And in the past week since I'd been practicing with the team, *never* was practically every fucking day.

The starting linebacker who'd just taken me down sneered at me. "You gonna play like shit, or be *the shit*? Get your shit together."

Shit. I coughed and got to my feet. He didn't offer me a hand, just turned away to hydrate. Coach had made me the second string quarterback two days ago, telling me not to make him regret it. I couldn't speak for him, but *I* definitely had some regrets. But I had no intention of showing my nerves to the team. They were already nipping at me, and I didn't want them to give me a reason to eat me alive.

A heavy hand fell on my left shoulder pad. "Hey, man, you good?"

As soon as I turned to see who was talking, my mouth went desert dry. "All good, bro," I said to Paul Martell, somehow managing to keep my cool.

"Rough hit." He frowned, his gaze assessing, stripping me bare. This wasn't a perfunctory look over for injuries; this was a full-on eye fuck.

"Yeah. I should've been ready for it." I gave him a wincing smile as I was finally able to take a deep breath. At least I could blame my red face on lack of oxygen.

"Probably." He shrugged, a grin tugging on the corners of his mouth. "Next time, you will be. Oh— and the nose of the ball's been down on your throws.

Loosen your grip. It's your first week, you're probably nervous AF, but you're letting it affect your throw. Unclench."

I sucked in another breath and nodded, face burning, both from attraction and disappointment in myself.

"Show me your form."

I nodded and picked up a ball. Deliberately relaxing, I channeled the unflappable QB who'd headed the small school's team I'd been on for a couple years.

Martell took off down the field, sprinting as though this were a championship game.

As soon as the ball left my hand, I focused on its trajectory. Perfect. His hands closed around the ball and he jogged it back, tossing it to me when he got close enough.

"See?" he said. "Relax. That was better."

"You gonna help me with that?" I replied, cocking an eyebrow.

"Just did."

*

A week—and more sore ribs—later, I was getting into a rhythm with the team. Though the drills were familiar, the intensity of the practices was something I'd never experienced, and if I wanted to close the gap between my current skills and where I needed to be, I had to up my game.

"Hey, dude, you got a sec?" I asked Martell as conditioning was winding down early one morning. Every day while we'd been suffering through agility training, I kept staring at him like my eyes had no choice but to be drawn in by his gravity. Watching as Martell's thick thighs pumped through high knees. Following as he dodged around cones and, later, defensemen, his calves flexing. Lithe body sprinting to make a catch.

But what I hadn't expected to see was Paul Martell's gray gaze staring right back in a "I want a verrry private, sweaty, clothing-free one-on-one workout with this new guy" way.

Fuck yeah. Feeling was mutual.

But now that I'd flagged him over, I had to keep it cool. *Pretend you don't want to dick him down.* Easier said than done.

"What's up?" His tongue slipped over his plush lips and my brain shorted out. *Focus.*

I shook my head and pushed sweaty blond waves out of my face. "You free? I could use some feedback on my pass—"

"Sorry, man. No time. Got PT in a few," he replied, already heading away. "Maybe tomorrow."

I tried not to let it get to me—after all, more than a few teammates had turned me down for extra practice—but it stung.

Not just the rejection, but the increasingly obvious difference between walk-ons and scholarship players.

The access to tutors, leniency from professors, the special meals…the list went on. I was a good student in general, and I could easily find time to read for my classes as an English major, but everything about this experience had me feeling like a green freshman all over again. The only thing keeping me going was that every time I pushed back when they gave me shit, I gained some yards toward their respect.

Instead of heading back to my sick new dorm, I stayed behind to do some passing drills with other second string players who had later classes. I needed to work ten times harder to prove myself. Starting now.

*

"Hey, Martell," I called out to him after Bernard the offensive coach outlined the drills we'd be doing. "What time do you get out of class today? There's this new sandwich place—"

"I'm following my meal plan today." He pinched the bridge of his nose.

"No worries," I said. "You wanna partner—"

"*I don't need you,*" Martell spit out and turned to walk toward Darryl Washington, our starting QB.

I watched him retreat, stunned. *What the fuck did I do?*

For the rest of the practice I concentrated on my form, my throws, the feel of the ball in my hands, anything to prevent thoughts about why Martell blew me off like I was nothing.

He's never really given you the time of day. What makes me think I'm anything to him other than nothing?

Though the number of times we caught each other staring said I was anything but.

*

"Oh no, it gets better," I said, trying to keep it together and finish telling the story to the group of Rams I was stretching with. "The poor kid was so turned around, not only did he run the wrong way, but when he reached the endzone, he puked all over the ref."

My teammates exploded in laughter and my face split in a wide grin. "Bro, I'd never show my face again," one of the linemen said, grabbing my shoulder as he left to get a drink.

Weeks had passed since I'd been made an official Ram, and I finally felt like one of them. Brutal conditioning, drills—the intense practices where I worked with the second string and closely with the starters in case I needed to fill in had slowly, brick by brick, built trust and camaraderie.

I got up to stretch my quads and noticed Paul Martell behind me, his deep gray eyes shooting daggers at the lineman who'd patted my arm. My stomach swooped, but I was sure I'd mistaken his expression. It was probably a cramp or something. It couldn't be jealousy.

*

The first games of the season came and went. Mom and I started a new book—a Regency romance between a sea captain and a vicar. Classes got more involved, papers written, tests taken, and Martell and I maintained the status quo. If it were even possible, Martell was *more* distant. Early on, he'd at least come over and show me how to improve a technique. Gave me pointers. Helped me navigate a play. But he'd pulled back completely, only acknowledging my presence as someone who threw him a ball once in a while.

If that.

His eyes stilled burned me though, turning my edges into embers.

That hadn't changed. I hadn't stopped watching him either.

No matter what I did, Martell seemed determined to just ignore me at best, hate me at worst. We even lived on the same goddamn floor—it was hard to avoid someone whose suite was two doors down the hall, but he managed. And I was fucking tired of it. The heat searing between us had to go somewhere before it ignited the atmosphere and, stupid as it was, it wasn't in my nature to just let it go.

Even if it was a hate-fuck to get it out of our systems.

As we'd headed into October, it seemed like it might stay as a hate-*eye*-fuck, at least from his end of things.

———

Goddamn locker room. And that fucking pass.

The stoplight turned red and I waited to cross the street, still a few blocks from the restaurant. I exhaled, the crisp fall evening fogging my breath. I should have been thinking about how well the day had gone, but Paul's words had stung more than I cared to admit. He'd insinuated that *I* had nearly cost them the game with my pass—the one *he* hadn't caught.

Bullshit.

I hated that I cared so much about what Paul Martell thought of me and how I played.

The light turned, and I pushed forward with the crowd again. I'd never had an opportunity to sub in like today. Not that I'd ever wish an injury on a teammate, but I'd had a chance to shine. That incomplete pass, though… not my fault. The internet and ESPN had supplied me with plenty of angles. It was Paul who'd fucked up, sprinting a split-second too late. This wasn't a mistake he'd made before. What the hell?

A strand of blond hair flew into my face and I roughly brushed it back, temper rising. The rest of the team had treated me just like one of them today. Everyone except Paul. What was so hard about just congratulating a teammate who'd played well? Or just not being an asshole?

I stopped in my tracks, still a block from the restaurant. Did he think I didn't belong with the rest of them? Was it because I wasn't on a scholarship? Did he disrespect me because I wasn't a starter?

"Fuck him," I said out loud, earning me a dirty look from a middle-aged woman standing within earshot. I had to know where I stood. It was one thing if he didn't like me or wasn't interested. But if Paul thought I hadn't earned my place on the team a hundred times over, he should have the balls to say it to my face.

Guessing that Paul had gone back to campus, I took out my phone and hailed a ride, then texted one of the guys to say I was exhausted and wasn't going to make it. By the time he hit me with a thumbs-up emoji, my ride was at the curb.

One minute I was getting in the car, the next it was pulling up in front of the new athlete housing complex. Modern lines and tinted windows loomed over me as I swiped my ID card to open the main doors.

The floors were relatively quiet, everyone out partying. Later, it'd be filled with enormous dudes with equally large hangovers, but for now, the silence suited what I needed to do.

I let myself into the common area of my suite and threw my jacket onto one of the sofas. After a few deep breaths, I headed out of my room and down the hall, pausing in front of Paul's suite, ready to knock.

Weird. The door was ajar but wasn't propped like he was waiting for someone. Whatever. With a deep breath, I entered.

"Martell? You here?" I called out. No response. "Hey, Paul?"

The whole team had been in and out of each other's suites over the past few months and I knew my way around, so once I'd navigated the sitting area I forked toward Paul's room. Like the front door, his was mostly closed, only allowing a faint line of light to escape.

A low moan followed the same path as the light, and I tensed. But it didn't sound quite like he was hurt.

I pushed the door open and walked in, gearing up to defend myself and give Paul a verbal ass-kicking.

But when my eyes adjusted to the light, I *wasn't* prepared for the scene in front of me.

Paul sat in an armchair angled slightly away from me, but he had headphones on. A laptop rested on his desk where a video played of two men fucking on cushioned patio furniture. One guy had messy, longer blond hair, and the other had dark hair and a deep tan.

Paul was completely naked, legs splayed wide, his sweatpants pooled on the floor. A full-length mirror gave me a side view my inner voyeur drooled over— one of his hands pinching a tight, furled nipple while the other caressed and teased the foreskin on his impressive cock. It smoothly slid with his hand's movements, the tip glistening as Paul swept his thumb over it, spreading a bead of liquid around.

Holy shit.

I couldn't look away.

"Mmm, Will. Just like that," Paul murmured. His breath hitched and his hips stuttered up just a little.

It took a second for his words to register in my rapidly short-circuiting brain, but when they did—

"*Fuck*," I said, maybe too sharply.

Paul's head snapped to the door where I stood against the frame. His face went ghost white. In one panicked motion, he leaned forward, threw his headphones on the bed, and slammed his laptop closed. Somehow he managed to grab his sweats from the floor and shoved them on to cover himself.

All I could do was stare.

Before he could say anything, I kicked the door closed the rest of the way and flicked the lock, filling the rest of the frame with my body.

Paul stood straight on shaky legs. Other than his blown-wide pupils, his expression was unreadable. Gone was the panic, replaced by…resignation?

"How long were you standing there?" Paul ground out.

I crossed my arms. "Long enough."

"Just fucking great." Paul barked a laugh and clenched his fists at his sides. "Why are you even here?"

"I—" My voice broke after the one syllable. "It doesn't matter."

"The hell it doesn't."

I shook my head, more to clear it than to answer him. Having Paul this close, this worked up, this *human*, was exhilarating. My mind was fuzzy, but I met Paul's fiery gray eyes straight on. "You said my name."

Paul's jaw hit the floor. "*What?*"

"Don't deny it. I heard you say—"

"No. No no no no no…" Paul wavered a little on his feet, the unsteadiness so unusual for someone so sure-footed on the field that it set off alarm bells. He swayed again, and I grabbed his biceps. Paul tightly wrapped long fingers around my forearm. "Fuck, yeah, okay. I said your fucking *name*. I was thinking about *you*," he said, defiantly raising his now nearly black eyes to mine. "Are you happy now? Shit, this can't get any wor—"

I took control and tilted his chin up with my other hand, leaned in, and pressed my lips to his, stealing his words straight from the source. The kiss was quick and close-mouthed, chaste by any standard, but it set my blood on fire.

Paul stared up at me, full lips slightly parted, and I had to force myself to not kiss him again.

"Now will you let me talk?" I asked, smiling slightly when Paul nodded.

Here goes nothing.

"You have no idea how many times I've done that *exact* same thing," I nodded toward his laptop, "just, you know, with the door locked." Paul's eyes widened and I closed mine. This absolutely wasn't how I'd expected this conversation to go, but there we were. I inhaled, breathing in the scent of aroused male and his body wash, preparing to let the universe sort it out. "Jesus, Paul, you're the hottest guy I've ever seen, and I never thought I'd have a chance with you. Ever."

"What?"

"I've seen you watching me. During practice, drills, conditioning. You *know* I've been watching you too. But you never responded to anything I did—and I thought my flirting was obvious—so I assumed you weren't interested."

Paul shook his head. "You—Will. I don't get involved with teammates. Seen it happen, too much drama. I told myself it would be better if I avoided you…"

Was I hearing him correctly? I scrunched my eyes and cocked my head. "Okay, to be clear—you were interested, but brushed me off because I'd be a *distraction*? I got no say in it?"

"Yeah." He snorted. "And the joke was on me—actually made it worse. I…shit. You're on my mind all the fucking time." Paul tilted his head back and drew in a sharp breath through his teeth. "The incomplete pass today was because I was watching you. Just a split-second too long, but…"

"Wow. Okay." I'd need to take some time processing *that* one. "And none of this is because I'm not on scholarship?" I pressed my lips into a thin line.

"No." Paul squeezed my arm. "I never gave a shit about that. What I said before—I'm sorry. For all of it."

I nodded, my brows knitting together. "So, you essentially took a page out of the douchebag little boy's pony-tail-pulling guide to letting someone know you liked them?"

Paul winced. "Yeah. I was an asshole."

"Yeah, you were. But…" I tightened my grip on his arm. He still hadn't let go of mine. "You had your reasons. I get it." I took a small step toward him. So close we were pressed together from abs to shoulder, so close the warmth radiated from his body, so close I could lick him if I wanted to. *Yes, please.* "But now, I totally want to hear you say my name again. Only louder."

CHAPTER
THREE

PAUL

AFTER HOLDING BACK FOR WEEKS, being this close to Will with my guard down went right to my head like a row of shots at Ted's Bar. I buried my face between Will's shoulder and neck, stopping before my mouth touched him. His scent surrounded me; whatever he'd used to shower after the game combined with good clean sweat. I reveled, unable to close the distance. If I did, the fantasy might disappear. But Will shifted, bringing his neck to my lips, and I groaned. The animal unleashed, I sucked over his strong jawline. The slight rasp of five o'clock shadow there roughed up my lips as I slid to his mouth.

Sensations hit me like a blind side tackle.

He leaned in again and I met him, pulling on his plump lower lip with my teeth. Will grunted, dirty and primal, and slipped his tongue between my lips. Fuck, if I'd thought he was distracting on the field, it didn't hold a candle to how he kissed. Like everything he did, Will threw himself into it. The attack and retreat of Will's mouth consumed me.

I shoved my palms up his chest, only to remember he was wearing far more clothing than I was. I trailed my fingers down the front of Will's tee to the hem and lifted the smooth cotton. He raised his arms and I helped him out of it, immediately getting my hands on his skin. I'd seen him shirtless just a couple hours before but getting to *touch* was a whole new level of torture. His pecs, carved by the months of training, were dusted lightly with hair, and flat brown nipples begged for my mouth.

Once I knew what he felt like, warm, bare, skin to skin, hot and hard and as desperate as I was, I'd never forget it. Hell, I may not remember anything else, ever.

I tilted my head away and Will chased my lips for a moment before his face fell in confusion, but his eyes blazed when I popped the button on his jeans. Taking the hint, he removed his pants and I guided him to sit on the armchair. I made to kneel down when Will stopped me with a hand on my hip.

"Your tests negative?" he asked.

It took me a second to realize he meant the STI tests done with the medical evaluations.

"Always have been," I replied.

"Good. Me too. Because I have to do something. Been dreaming of it. But stop me if you don't want it," he said.

"I have a feeling I'd like just about *anything* you want to do."

Will shifted to the edge of the cushion and licked his lips before sliding his index finger into the waistband of my sweatpants to pull me forward. With a wicked grin, he pressed his face against the bulging outline of my hard cock through my pants, mouthing the fabric. His bright green eyes were glued to mine as he slowly, carefully, deliberately licked the wet spot where I'd leaked through the soft gray cotton. My brain shorted out and my thighs tensed and trembled with the effort to not rock into his face.

In a flash, my sweats were down to my knees, cool air hitting my flushed skin for a moment before Will took my cock in his mouth.

My world narrowed to the sensation of his warm mouth on my body, and I ran my fingers through his wavy hair. Will groaned low in his throat as he slid his tongue around the sensitive ridge of my head, then spread the wetness over his lips until they shone. His eyes had glazed over like he'd transcended to another plane of existence just from sucking my cock. I tightly grasped the base of the shaft, wresting back a semblance of control.

"Do you like this?" Will asked. He reached up with one hand and circled his fingers around the middle of my shaft, moving my foreskin up and down slightly. It glided, soaked with my precum and his saliva, slipping without any friction. His tongue circled the head once and retreated, a teasing eyebrow raised. "Well?"

"Yes! God, yes," I said, finally remembering how to speak.

"Good." He jacked me off with one hand, head bobbing enthusiastically as he took the tip in his mouth over and over. My hips jerked forward of their own volition, my cock hitting the back of his throat. Will pulled off. Had I hurt him?

"Do that again," he said, and electricity danced along my skin. I did, desperate for more, letting him control the depth.

His other hand trailed to my thigh, scratching through the hair there with his short nails, then over to my balls, leaving trails of fire. His throat constricted around me, hot and velvet, but his green eyes staring up into mine was what made me blush. He tugged my sack before one finger strayed to the sensitive patch of skin behind them. But he didn't move.

I widened my stance as much as I could with my pants around my knees, wordlessly encouraging him. Will's mouth left my dick just long enough to lick a finger, which he pressed lightly against my hole. He didn't push inside but worked the little knot of muscle in a tiny, slick circle. I shivered, the intimacy overwhelming, and I almost pulled away. It had been so long since I'd been with anyone I trusted. When I first saw him in my room, just standing there, I'd been terrified. But there was no judgment; only acceptance and more enthusiasm than I ever could have hoped for. Our connection sizzled, pure fantasy come to life.

I dragged my fingers though his longish hair as the pleasure climbed on the right side of too much, too good, too sensitive. "Will," I panted. "Oh—"

Our eyes met again, and he hummed, deep and resonant, the vibrations hurrying my climax. Will pulled back, just enough to keep my swollen cockhead between his lips. A slick tongue danced over my sensitive flesh, dipping into the slit at the tip and darting around the rest, teasing until I spilled in greedy pulses into his welcoming mouth. He groaned, eyes fluttering shut, and I melted.

Will swallowed around me, then relaxed his jaw, letting me slip out as I began to soften in his hand. A final spurt caught him on his lips, and he mirrored what he'd done earlier, gently dragging the oversensitive head through the creamy wetness there.

"Fuck, so good," I murmured, cupping his cheek with a hand and rubbing my thumb over the corner of his lips before bringing it to my mouth and tasting us, sweet and salty. Meant to go together, like bacon and eggs, peanut butter and chocolate, milk and cookies. A perfect combo on the field, and even better in the bedroom.

"Jesus, Paul," he mumbled, eyes closed.

I grinned and pushed Will back on the chair, stripped his underwear off, and straddled his thighs. Will's skin was flushed and sweaty, his lips swollen and open, the picture of debauchery and I'd barely touched him yet.

Unable to resist, I dove back in to taste myself again. I breathed him in. Arousal still pooled deep, but the fire had banked to something slow and languid. This time it wasn't about me.

I ran one hand up Will's arm to the side of his neck, cupped the damp skin, traced his sharp jawline. With the other, I skimmed down his firm body. Muscles jumped in his stomach as my hand descended to his cock. It twitched when I brushed it with my fingertips, standing straight and proud and wet as anything against his abs. A firm stroke was rewarded as a clear bead pearled on the deep-red crown. Will had to be *aching*.

"What do you want?" I whispered, settling more of my weight on his firm thighs. When he tried to thrust into my grip, abs flexing, I chuckled and stilled.

"Anything." Will swallowed thickly, throat working, and my mind went immediately to how he'd felt surrounding me, swallowing. "Anything you want to give me."

"What I want," I said, brushing my fingertips over the short coarse hair at the base of his cock, "is to make. You. Fucking. Lose. It."

I shifted to grind our bodies together, capturing his mouth in a filthy kiss, more tongue and moans than finesse. I wasn't hard again yet, but he painted a dirty trail across my stomach, slick and enticing.

"Oh yeah, please. Make me come." Will grabbed the chair arms with shaking hands, then dragged his hands up my thighs, digging his fingers into the meat of my hips to keep me close.

I kissed him again, full of promise.

Will nodded, his eyes glossy, and pulled away for only as long as it took me to lick my palm and take him in hand again, smoothing the gentle up-down motions and coaxing more precum from him. I drew a slippery finger around the ridge of his cockhead, torturing the delicate skin and enjoying the way Will's abs contracted as he fought every instinct to *take* instead of letting me *give*.

Making Will fall apart was a play I hadn't run before, but I was an expert in watching him. He bit his lip when I gave him quick, short strokes. Threw his head back and full-on wailed when I twisted my hand over the head. Tilted his chin up, mouth pouty, searching for my lips when I tugged gently on his balls.

And when his whole body pulled taut as a bowstring, eyes barely open, mouth lax, little panting breaths escaping at ragged intervals—that's when I knew I'd made the right play. Thick pulses streamed down his shaft and over my fingers, so much better than any fantasy.

Breathing like he'd run sprints, Will wrapped his arms around my waist, drawing me close. Neither of us cared about the mess. I was an idiot, thinking I should deny myself—deny us—what our bodies wanted. And our hearts, the little voice in my head added, and I couldn't deny that, either. I exhaled hard, and Will shivered, laughing.

"We definitely should have done that sooner," Will said.

"Yeah," I said. "And we definitely need to do it again." I threaded my fingers into the blond hair at the back of Will's neck and tipped his head to have better access to his mouth.

Will hummed, sliding his hands down to my lower back, teasing the split of my cheeks for a moment before adjusting his grip. He got up and the ground tilted as he lifted me. I shouted in surprise, but it turned into a low laugh when I pictured him shoving me up against a door or holding me down on the bed, pressing me against the shower wall, trapping my wrists behind me, gripping the back of my neck as he slid his cock into—

"Let's clean up," he said.

"Then we can get dirty again?"

"That's the plan." His flirty wink turned my legs to jelly. Good thing he had a firm hold on me. As though reading my mind, Will set me down and followed me into my private bathroom.

"Think we can make this work?" I grabbed his ass, then turned the shower on.

Will snorted. "I think we're making it work pretty well already. But the team'll probably wonder what took us so long. We made a nice recovery though, right?"

I laughed. "Only after an epic fumble."

Will's face broke into a sassy grin. "You mean incomplete pass." He wiggled his eyebrows as he led me into the steam. "But this time, it's a fair catch."

ACKNOWLEDGMENTS

As always, thank you to my husband for being my best cheerleader. I love you!

Thank you to Beth Bolden for all the amazing advice and feedback.

Thank you to Passionate Ink for creating another amazing anthology, where this story first featured.

Thank you to the Red Reines for making the tastiest sausage.

And thank you to my readers, who make it all worthwhile.

ABOUT THE AUTHOR

Ryley Banks writes award-winning bestselling spicy romance, mostly of the LGBTQ+ variety. She's a connoisseur of tea and gin and loves language, especially creative profanity.

When she's not begging her characters to behave or reading fanfic, you can find Ryley watching cooking how-to videos, traveling, or, if you're lucky, crafting the next story to make you smile and set you on fire.

Stay up to date on all of Ryley's releases and more by subscribing to her VIP reader newsletter. Subscribers receive a free novelette, *Heat Waves*.

https://ryleybanks.com/ryleys-vip-newsletter/

Visit Ryley at: https://ryleybanks.com/

facebook.com/RyleyBAuthor

instagram.com/ryleybauthor

bookbub.com/authors/ryleybanks

goodreads.com/ryleybanks

ALSO BY RYLEY BANKS

Find all of Ryley's books:

Or go to: https://ryleybanks.com/books/

The Big Bad Book of Bedtime Stories

(erotic short stories)

Eggplant Night

Dirty Dishes

Teacher Pet

Third Time's the Charm

Anthologies

The Big Book of Orgasms Volume 2: 69 Sexy Stories (featuring *Third Time's the Charm*)

Ink: Queer Sci Fi's Eighth Annual Flash Fiction Contest (featuring *Right Place, Right Time*)

Nonfiction

Demystifying the Beats: How to Write a Killer Book by Carol Potenza, Jordyn Kross, Ryley Banks, and Erin Krueger

HEAT WAVES

HEAT WAVES: A SPICY MM
KRAKEN SHIFTER MONSTER
ROMANCE

The king will have his elven mate in his arms again—all eight of them—no matter the cost.

Woodland elf Kalysin is thrust into a riptide of dreams as a dangerous drought parches the land. Stolen memories of a bronzed muscled figure who bathed him in ecstasy, but disappeared back into the sea, gone forever.

Could the dreams bubbling up from forgotten depths have anything to do with the shadowy stalker in the forests surrounding his liege's orchards and withering fields of crops? Or have they been stirred up by an evil magic that threatens famine and starvation across the lands? When Kal is forced to make a sacrifice to save his mother, will he survive long enough to be reclaimed by his mate? Or will the real monster doom him to take his memories to the grave?

Keep reading for an exclusive excerpt from *Heat Waves*, now available for free!

EXCERPT FROM HEAT WAVES

THE ELF'S whisper-quiet steps should have kept him well hidden. And they would—but not from me. His long brown hair was swept back and tied out of his way. My mouth watered. What if I gave in to the urge to sink my pointed canines into his neck, dragging them down the flesh to hear him cry out? My body tensed, eager to take take *take*. No. It wasn't time. But soon, he'd remember he belonged to me.

———

"Did you see that?" I froze, my long fingers stretched toward a low hanging bunch of nectar fruit. I gestured with my chin. "Over there."

Vulen, my assistant, turned his gaze toward the tree line. Nothing moved, though I was certain I'd seen an unnatural shadow. "I'm sorry, Kalysin. I must have missed it." His gray eyes swept back to me. "Perhaps you should have a drink of water. It's been so hot and dry—"

"I'm fine"—*absolutely not hallucinating, or insane, or seeing things*—"unlike these nectar fruit. They should be smooth, shiny. A vibrant green. But this whole orchard is sickly." I touched the cluster of fruit, and half of them dropped to the ground, joining countless others. I picked up several and gave them to Vulen, who labeled and packed them away for inspection.

Lord Elmar had demanded I meet with him that morning about the crops. I'd rushed in late, meeting Vulen at the door. Lord Elmar had been in his conservatory.

"What am I giving you coin for, Kalysin, as my Overseer of Lands, if you don't actually *oversee*?" He clenched a freshly picked furry yellow fruit in his hand so hard the fruit's skin began to split, separating from the flesh. "Consequences, Kalysin, and dire ones, if this continues—your tardiness and the deteriorating harvest. You should be able to do *something* since your own lands are producing. We all must make sacrifices." He dropped the mangled fruit, and it hit the marble floor with a muffled wet thud. A servant swept in and cleaned up every trace.

I'd bowed in acquiescence, unwilling to brave Lord Elmar's reaction if I told him the reason I was late was because his messenger had notified me at an ungodly early hour, and I'd arrived as soon as I could.

As Vulen and I finished with the nectar fruit orchard, taking a few more samples, I panicked over what to tell Lord Elmar. What were samples of crops going to show, other than the simple fact the plants weren't getting enough water?

"We're going to the brambleberries next?" Vulen asked, adjusting his water packs.

"Yes." Lord Elmar had also made it clear our rate of crop monitoring was unsatisfactory. "I don't want another meeting like this morning's if we can help it."

"I was afraid he would strike you," Vulen whispered as we made our way across Lord Elmar's vast lands to the next planted plot, our sandaled feet kicking up a plume of dust behind us as though the ground didn't remember what it was like to be wet.

"Me too," I admitted. "But it's no matter. I'm fortunate Lord Elmar gave me a position other than as a servant or messenger." Or so I kept reminding myself.

The brambleberry bushes were planted in interminably long tracts. We settled under a scrubby tree that provided some shade about halfway down one of the lines. Vulen removed the packs he carried and wiped the sweat from his forehead. I drank from my water-skin, half empty already. I swallowed, then knelt in the sandy dirt, peering under the lowest brambleberry branches. A concerning number of hard, green-white fruit. After carefully plucking two of the few ripe black ones, I offered Vulen one and popped the other in my mouth. The sweet, tangy juice rushed over my tongue, and I closed my eyes, taking brief joy in one of the few perks of my work. I hummed, transported back to my time as a youngling, raiding my mother's brambleberry bushes with— My brows knit together. I couldn't recall my playmate's features, much less their name.

But the headache I had from the effort to remember was very real indeed. They'd been happening increasingly often, as were the dreams slipping through my mind like a handful of seawater as soon as I woke each morning.

"Are you well, Kalysin?" Vulen asked, his head tilted to the side.

"No. This damned heat." I spit out a seed that had lodged in my teeth. "Let's get this over with."

We trudged onward, the top branches of the long, staked rows of thorny bushes repeating the same story as the lower ones with the addition of curled, sun-scorched leaves.

"Do you remember when it last rained?" I asked Vulen.

He frowned. "I—maybe late spring? Or perhaps it was early spring." Vulen stared off in the distance, over the rolling hills and the cloudless blue sky.

"I can't remember either," I admitted. The rains had not come this summer to fill the streams and rivers to bursting like they had in the past, yet I'd held out hope the drought hadn't affected the crops. Between the brambleberries, the nectar fruit earlier, and the sickly patches of spike melons we'd inspected before them, this was nothing like I'd ever seen.

The midday summer sun burned my tanned arms, but my skin prickled as though a winter chill had blown in. Someone was watching me.

Not us.

Me.

Continue reading *Heat Waves* by Ryley Banks, available for free on BookFunnel.

Copyright © 2023 by Ryley Banks

THE BIG BAD BOOK OF BEDTIME STORIES

SHORT, SPICY, STEAMY READS TO KEEP YOU UP.

Eggplant Night: A Why Choose Romance

He'll make her fantasy come true.

Jax and Bree have a weekly date night, marked with a certain emoji on their shared calendar. They've done a lot as a couple—axe throwing, cooking classes, outdoor concerts—but tonight is different. This time, date night's a group activity.

Eggplant Night is a FMMMM+ romantic erotica short story of about 5,000 words.

Keep reading for an excerpt from *Eggplant Night*, now available at your favorite online retailer!

EXCERPT FROM EGGPLANT NIGHT

"BREE?"

Jax stroked a hand down the back of my head, raking through my wavy, dark hair until my spine was liquid. After not nearly long enough, he placed a mug down in front of me and sat in his spot across the oak kitchen table with a steaming mug of his own. Then he blushed and began to shred a napkin. I cocked an eyebrow. Whatever it was, this was going to be good.

Since he so clearly needed a moment to gather his thoughts, I took a swig of hot coffee and finished typing an appointment in my phone's calendar app, eyes flicking to our weekly Friday night date. I'd started marking it with an eggplant emoji years ago, and I smiled at the silly—and sexy—reminder. Then I put my phone down to give him, and the coffee, my full attention.

"What's on your mind?" I scooted forward and met his gaze.

"Remember…remember our conversation a few months ago?"

Did I *ever*. Prompted by a friend's shocking affair, we'd spent an entire evening, and more wine than I cared to admit, confessing our deepest fantasies to each other. Even though we'd been married a decade, apparently we hadn't even scratched the surface—but when you bind yourself to someone for *forever*, no one outright tells you that neither of you are mind-readers and you need to talk about that shit.

"Uh huh," I said neutrally and sipped my drink. I watched him under my downcast eyelashes as he psyched himself up to continue. If possible, he was even more handsome than when we first got together. Fuck our twenties. Mid-thirties looked better and better.

An email notification chirped on my phone; I silenced it and tossed it onto the third chair. Jax would always come first.

"Would you be up for doing something a little different for date night this week?" he asked.

We'd done everything from the classic dinner-and-a-movie to escape rooms and axe throwing. "Sure. Have something in mind?"

Jax met my eyes over his coffee cup. "When you went for your physical last month, did they send you a copy of your STI test?"

Huh?

If his goal was to keep me off-balance, he was knocking it out of the park. "Yeah. All negative, of course." I tilted my head, curiosity officially piqued. "Jax, what's this—"

"Bree—were you serious about doing some of what we discussed?"

My mouth went dry, the list replaying in my mind in all its taboo glory. Nothing we'd talked about that evening was off-limits, at least with some serious discussion first. But *some* fantasies…

Game on.

I took his hand and squeezed. "Only if it's together. And safe."

"Good. I was hoping we were still on the same page," he said. "Because I might—*might*—have found a way to make one of yours—and mine—come true."

"What?" My heart thundered so hard I was afraid it would crack my ribs open. "Which one?" Anticipation of the unknown racked me with shivers.

Jax shook his head. "Nothing's final. But…" He got up and pulled an unassuming manila folder off the counter and set it in front of me. The chair creaked as he sat again. "I needed to make sure you were fully on board."

Jax opened the folder and tapped a blank line next to one he'd already signed. "Your signature." He licked his lips. "Do you trust me?"

He was earnest, honest, and, most importantly, mine.

My answer came as easy as breathing. "With my life."

With how quickly I moved the pen, I was surprised my signature didn't catch the paper on fire.

Some husbands surprised their wives with flowers.

Some husbands surprised their wives with chocolate.

Some husbands, apparently, surprised their wives with a night of exploring their deepest fantasies together.

Fuck, am I lucky.

Don't miss *Eggplant Night* by Ryley Banks, available now wherever books are sold.

Copyright © 2024 by Ryley Banks

RYLEY'S VIP READER LIST

Sign up for Ryley's VIP reader list and get a free copy of *Heat Waves*, along with her latest new release news, updates, deals, freebies, and giveaways!

Or go to: https://www.ryleybanks.com/ryleys-vip-newsletter